51 x 9/19 -B
56 x 5/23

JE CHACONAS
Chaconas, Dori,
Cork and Fuzz :the babysitters /

CORK & FUZZ

The Babysitters

A Viking Easy-to-Read

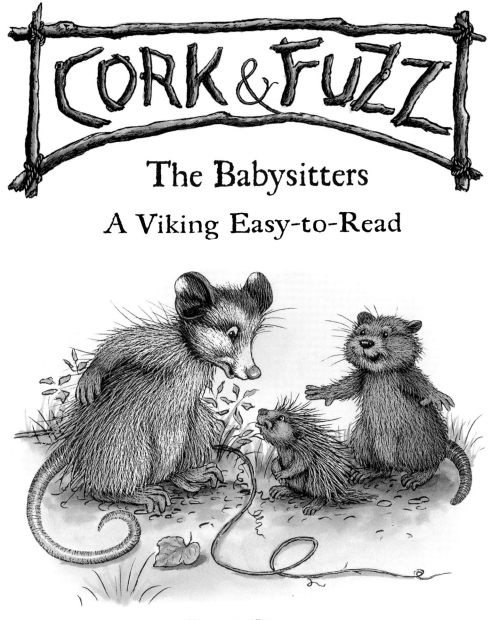

by **Dori Chaconas**
illustrated by **Lisa McCue**

Alameda Free Library
1550 Oak Street

AN IMPRINT OF PENGUIN GROUP (USA) INC.

VIKING
Published by Penguin Group
Penguin Young Readers Group, 345 Hudson Street, New York, New York 10014, U.S.A.
Penguin Group (Canada), 90 Eglinton Avenue East, Suite 700, Toronto, Ontario, Canada M4P 2Y3
(a division of Pearson Penguin Canada Inc.)
Penguin Books Ltd, 80 Strand, London WC2R 0RL, England
Penguin Ireland, 25 St Stephen's Green, Dublin 2, Ireland (a division of Penguin Books Ltd)
Penguin Group (Australia), 250 Camberwell Road, Camberwell, Victoria 3124, Australia
(a division of Pearson Australia Group Pty Ltd)
Penguin Books India Pvt Ltd, 11 Community Centre, Panchsheel Park, New Delhi – 110 017, India
Penguin Group (NZ), 67 Apollo Drive, Rosedale, North Shore 0632, New Zealand
(a division of Pearson New Zealand Ltd)
Penguin Books (South Africa) (Pty) Ltd, 24 Sturdee Avenue, Rosebank, Johannesburg 2196,
South Africa

Penguin Books Ltd, Registered Offices: 80 Strand, London WC2R 0RL, England

First published in 2010 by Viking, a division of Penguin Young Readers Group

1 3 5 7 9 10 8 6 4 2

LIBRARY OF CONGRESS CATALOGING-IN-PUBLICATION DATA
Chaconas, Dori, date–
Cork and Fuzz : the babysitters / by Dori Chaconas ; illustrated by
Lisa McCue.
p. cm.
Summary: Cork the muskrat tries to persuade his best friend Fuzz,
a possum, to help babysit for a porcupine.
ISBN 978-0-670-01200-8 (hardcover)
[1. Babysitters—Fiction. 2. Opossums—Fiction. 3. Muskrat—Fiction.
4. Porcupines—Fiction. 5. Best friends—Fiction. 6. Friendship—Fiction.]
I. McCue, Lisa, ill. II. Title. III. Title: Babysitters.
PZ7.C342Cos 2010
[E]—dc22
2009030386

Viking ® and Easy-to-Read ® are registered trademarks of Penguin Group (USA) Inc.

Manufactured in China   Set in Bookman

Chapter One

Cork was a short muskrat.

He liked to help.

He liked to help baby birds.

He liked to help keep the pond clean.

Fuzz was a tall possum.

He liked to help, too.

He liked to help himself to worms for breakfast.

He liked to help himself to trash-bin scraps for supper.

Two best friends. One was helpful. The other one was Fuzz.

One day Cork walked to Fuzz's house.
He walked slowly. He walked slowly
because he was holding a baby porcupine
by the paw.

Fuzz was in his yard. He was pulling
leaves off a long vine.

"What are you doing?" Cork asked.

"I am busy," Fuzz said. "Where did you
find the pokie-pie?"

"I did not find him," Cork said. "His mother gave him to me."

"To keep?" Fuzz asked.

"Not to keep," Cork said. "I am helping. I am babysitting."

Fuzz looked at the porcupine. "I would not

want to babysit on him," Fuzz said.

"I would get poked with a pokie."

"No, no, no," Cork said. "Babysit does not

mean you sit on the baby. It means you

watch him."

"Erk!" said the baby porcupine. He picked

up a stone. He put it in his mouth.

"Watch him eat stones?" Fuzz asked.

Cork took the stone out of the baby's

mouth.

"Watch him so he does not get hurt," Cork

said. "Will you help me babysit?"

"Not today," Fuzz said. "I am busy making

a bear trap."

Chapter Two

"What will you do with the bear when you trap it?" Cork asked.

"First I will trap the bear," Fuzz said. "Then I will think about what to do with it."

Fuzz made a loop with the vine. He laid
the loop on the ground.

"Erk!" said the baby porcupine. He put
a flower in his mouth.

Cork took the flower out of the baby's
mouth. "Help me, Fuzz!" he said.

"I am busy," Fuzz said.

Fuzz put a large rock on the vine next to the loop.

"Erk!" said the porcupine. He put a pinecone in his mouth.

Cork took the pinecone out of the baby's mouth.

"Please, Fuzz!" Cork said. "I really need your help!"

"I am very, very busy," Fuzz said.

Fuzz climbed a tree. He crawled to the end of a branch. The branch bent down and down and down. Fuzz tied the loose end of the vine to the tip of the branch.

"Erk!" said the porcupine. He put some tree bark in his mouth.

Cork took the bark out of the baby's mouth. "Please, please, please, Fuzz!" he said. "If you help me babysit, I will give you my best green stone."

"Okay," said Fuzz. He held out his paw for

the stone. "I was done anyway."

"Ack! Ack! Ack!" The baby porcupine stuck

out his tongue. Then he started to cry.

"He is chewing a bitter berry," Fuzz said.

"Please do not cry!" Cork said. He took the bitter berry out of the baby's mouth. Then he wiped the porcupine's tongue with his paw.

"ACK! ACK! ACK!" The porcupine cried louder.

"Now he has got muskrat fur on his tongue," Fuzz said.

"Help me, Fuzz," Cork said. "Help me make him stop crying!"

Chapter Three

"Okay," said Fuzz. "I will help. I will stand on my head."

"How will that help?" Cork asked.

"It will help because I do not know how to stand on my head," Fuzz said. "I will fall over. The pokie-pie will stop crying and he will laugh."

Fuzz stood on his head. He fell over.

The baby did not stop crying.

"That did not help," Cork said.

"I will sing him a song," Fuzz said.

"Do you know a song?" Cork asked.

"I will make one up," Fuzz said.

"Hey pokie-pokies.

The cat told some jokies.

The cow jumped in the lagoon."

"That does not make any sense,"

Cork said.

The baby cried even louder.

"I will do a step-kick dance for him," Fuzz said.

"I will step with one foot. I will kick with the other foot."

Fuzz stepped on the grass. He kicked a weed. He stepped on the path. He kicked a daisy. Then he stepped in the vine loop. He kicked the large stone.

The stone rolled. The vine loop grabbed Fuzz's foot.

WHOOSH!

Fuzz hung upside down in the tree.

"Help!" Fuzz yelled.

"You caught yourself in the bear trap!"
Cork said.

The baby porcupine stopped crying. He
clapped his paws. He waved at Fuzz.
Then he laughed.

"Help me, Cork!" Fuzz yelled. "Climb up
the tree. Untie the vine!"

"Muskrats cannot climb trees!" Cork
said. "And I have to watch the pokie-pie."
Cork looked down at the porcupine.

"Oh no!" Cork said.

Chapter Four

Cork could not see the baby anywhere.

"Help me!" Fuzz yelled.

"I want to help you," Cork called up to Fuzz. "But I have to find the baby! Can you see him from up there?"

"Yes," Fuzz said. "I can see the pokie-pie."

"Is he in the bushes?" Cork asked.

"No," Fuzz said.

"Is he in the tall grass?" Cork asked.

"No," Fuzz said.

Cork stamped his foot.

"Just tell me where he is!" Cork yelled.

"He is right up here," Fuzz said.

Cork looked up. The baby porcupine was crawling out on the tree branch. "Pokie-pie!" Cork yelled. "Come down here!"

The porcupine crawled to the end of the branch. He grabbed the vine. He chewed and chewed and chewed. He chewed right through the vine.

"YEOW!" Fuzz fell into the bitter berry bush.

"I am taking the pokie-pie back to his mother,"
Cork said. "I am not a good babysitter."

"You are a good babysitter," Fuzz said. "You
even taught the pokie-pie to be a good helper."

"I did?" Cork asked.

"Yes. He helped me get out of the trap."

Cork smiled. "Then I do not feel so bad," he said.

"Now I am the only one who feels bad," Fuzz said.

"Why do you feel bad?" Cork asked.

Fuzz answered, "Because I did not catch a bear."

Cork patted Fuzz on the back. "We can sing, if
it will make you feel better."

31

And so they did. Two best friends, singing and swinging the porcupine home.

"There was a baby pokie-pie
with pokies on his back-back-back.
He put a berry in his mouth,
and stuck his tongue out. Ack-ack-ack!"